Time to Wake Up!

MARISABINA RUSSO

 Greenwillow Books, New York

**With love for my son
Samuel Travis Williams Stark**

Gouache paints were used for the full-color art.
The text type is Humanist 521.
Copyright © 1994 by Marisabina Russo Stark
All rights reserved. No part of this book may
be reproduced or utilized in any form or by
any means, electronic or mechanical, including
photocopying, recording, or by any information
storage and retrieval system, without permission
in writing from the Publisher, Greenwillow Books,
a division of William Morrow & Company, Inc.,
1350 Avenue of the Americas, New York, NY 10019.
Printed in Hong Kong by South China Printing
Company (1988) Ltd.
First Edition   10 9 8 7 6 5 4 3 2 1

Library of Congress Cataloging-in-Publication Data

Russo, Marisabina.
Time to wake up / by Marisabina Russo.
    p.   cm.
Summary: A mother has some
difficulty getting her little boy
out of bed in the morning.
ISBN 0-688-04599-5 (trade).
ISBN 0-688-04600-2 (lib. bdg.)
[1. Morning — Fiction.
2. Mother and child — Fiction.]
I. Title.   PZ7.R9192Ti   1994   [E] — dc20
93-18185   CIP   AC

Time to wake up!

I can't wake up.

Open your eyes.

Can I open just one?

A good-morning kiss.

Teddy wants me to stay.

Off with your quilt.

No, it's so warm and cozy.

I'll tickle your toes.

I'll tickle your nose.

Up on two feet.

I think I'll walk on four.

Now it's time to get dressed.

I want my truck shirt.

I'll be right back.

Zzzzzzzzzzzzzzzzz.

You fooled me.

My bowl and my spoon.

And a lunch bag for school.

You're taking too long.

Now I'm ready.

Good-bye, Mama.

Good-bye, Sam.